MAXIMUM VOLUME

BY SIRO
TRANSLATED BY MICHELA NONIS
EDITED BY DEBRA RABAS
LETTERED BY ADAM KUBERT
COVER DESIGN AND
INTERIOR PRODUCTION
BY JO YARDLEY

Originally published by Zenda Editions, Paris.
North American English language edition © 1994 Kitchen Sink Press, Inc. All rights reserved.
Previously published as *Master Volume* in *Heavy Metal* ® magazine. *Maximum Volume* is
published by Kitchen Sink Press, Inc., 320 Riverside Drive, Northampton, MA
01060, by arrangement with *Heavy Metal* magazine. *Heavy Metal* is a registered trademark of Metal Mammoth, Inc. Kitchen Sink is a registered
trademark of Kitchen Sink Press, Inc. Contents © 1992
Zenda/Siro. All rights reserved. No part of this book can
be reproduced without written permission of the
copyright holders, except short excerpts for
review or other journalistic purposes.
ISBN 0-87816-281-X
Printed in U.S.A.

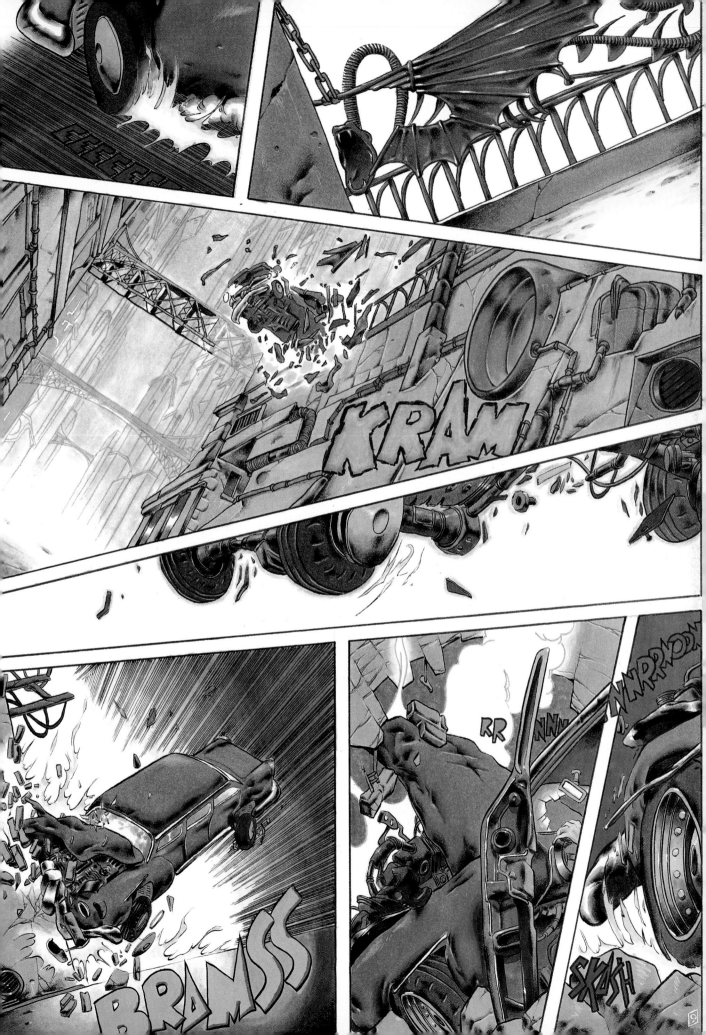

COULD THERE BE AN ABERRATION OF VIRGINAL WHITE ON THE OTHER SIDE OF NOWHERE...

I TRY TO CONVINCE MYSELF THAT SOMETHING SO PURE DOESN'T EXIST. BUT SINCE THAT ORANGE MONSTER...

INJECTED THAT VISION IN MY BRAIN...

I CANNOT GET RID OF MY ANGUISH.

WE GOT THE LIMO.

WAS IT THEIR CAR?

IT BECAME THEIR HEARSE.

BUT THE JOURNALIST WASN'T IN IT.

NO, NOT THE SLIGHTEST IDEA. REALLY, YOU CAN'T BELIEVE IT WAS AN ATTEMPT ON MY LIFE--I HAVE NO ENEMIES...

...BUT LET'S GET DOWN TO BUSINESS...

KWO PL

WHA THA

OH, THAT POOR MAN JUST LOST HIS WIFE. WELL...

YOU UNDERSTAND... THE SHOCK OF IT ALL. HE JUST COULDN'T DEAL WITH IT.

THE SHOCK. OF COURSE...HEM...LET'S SEE...WHAT I REALIZED LOOKING THROUGH YOUR PRESS CLIPS IS THAT VERY LITTLE IS KNOWN ABOUT YOUR PRIVATE LIFE...

A FEW DETAILS. NOTHING REALLY ARRESTING. LET'S SEE, WHAT WOULD BE THE BEST WAY TO DESCRIBE YOU?

ABSTRACTED. OMNIPRESENT, LIKE GOD. WITH SEVERAL RIGHT ARMS, LIKE THE BUDDHA, WHOSE COLOR YOU ALSO WEAR...

PEOPLE LIKE YOU PRIDE THEMSELVES IN MAKING UP LEGENDS. BUT YOU MUST KNOW THAT IT'S NOT THE WEATHER VANE THAT TURNS, IT'S THE WIND.

WHAT ELSE? YOU HATE TOBACCO AND ALCOHOL, EXCEPT FOR A LEMON ALCOHOL CALLED THE SPYROFIZZ...YOUR POWERS OF SEDUCTION ARE LEGENDARY AND ACCORDING TO WHAT SOME ARTICLES SAY, YOU ALSO POSSESS SUPERNATURAL POWERS.

WELL, ARE THESE LEGENDS OR THE TRUTH?

ZAPP

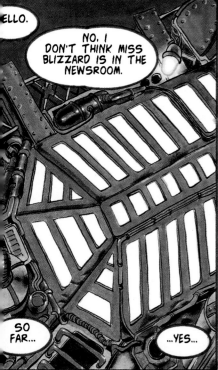

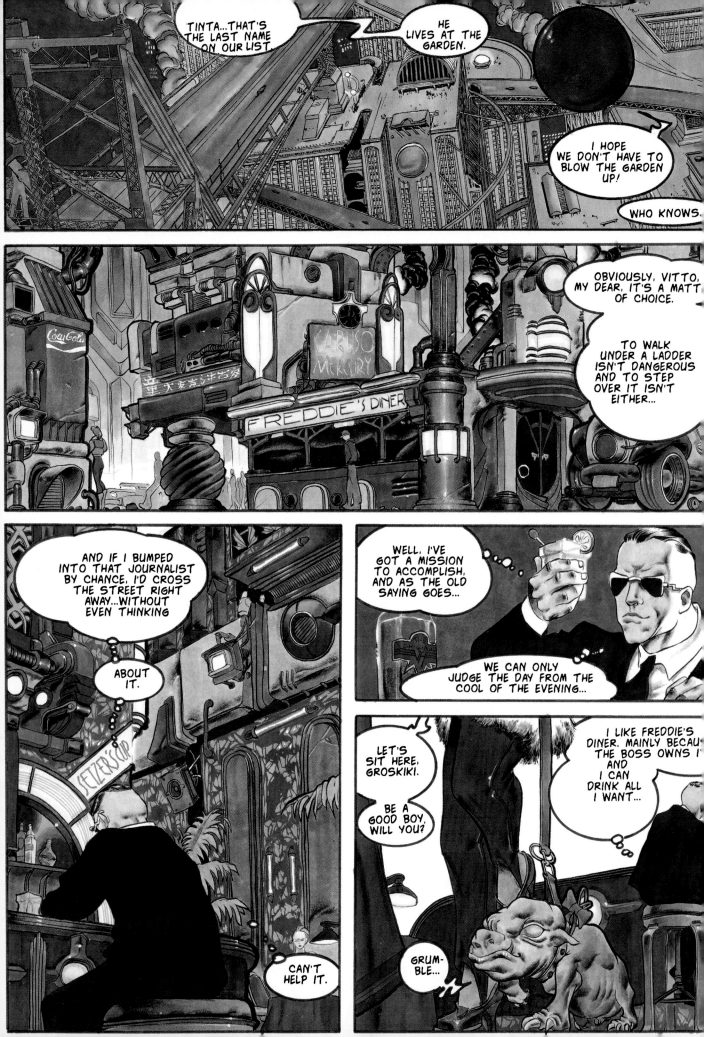

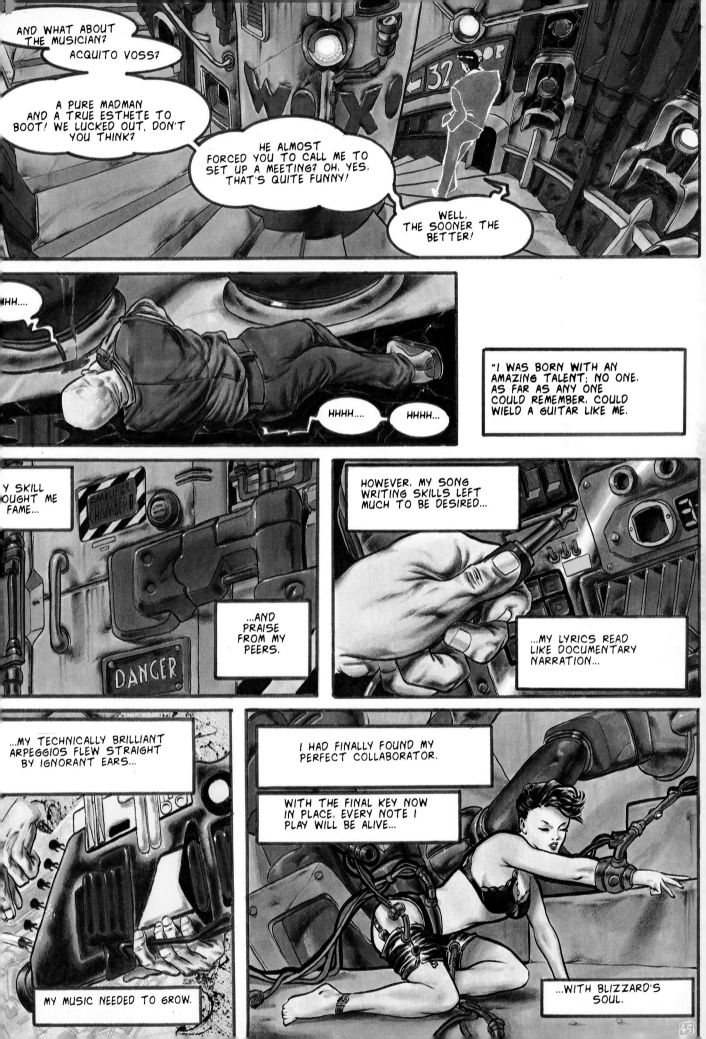

FROM COMIC BOOKS TO MOVIES AND SATURDAY MORNING CARTOONS!

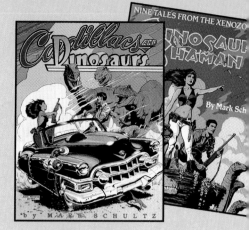

THE CROW COLLECTED by James O'Barr

For some things there is no forgiveness! A grim tale of love, tragedy, and revenge beyond death as Eric returns to avenge the brutal murder of his fiancée. A violent, bloody retribution.

The Crow has kept thousands of readers enthralled since its debut in 1989. Now all previously printed material is collected in this 232-page book including all-new full-color cover, 8-page color section of the original Caliber and Tundra covers, several previously unpublished pieces of spot artwork, two stories, "Inertia" and "Atmosphere", not found in the three volume series, and a very special dedication to Brandon Lee who recently lost his life in the final days of filming *The Crow* movie.

232pp, softcover, Mature Readers, $15.95

CADILLACS AND DINOSAURS™ by Mark Schultz

This award-winning comic book series comes to Saturday morning TV fall on CBS. Three graphic novels collect all of the original stories ● future time when all past ages meet. The world within these pages is where time is out of kilter. The human race is reduced to a despe● struggle to stay alive. Dinosaurs roam the plains with Cadillacs and people — Jack "Cadillac" Tenrec and Hannah Dundee — search answers to the puzzles of the age.

Cadillacs and Dinosaurs™, Collected Volume 1, 136pp, softcover, $14.●
Dinosaur Shaman, Collected Volume 2, 128pp, softcover, $14.95
Time in Overdrive, Collected Volume 3, 128pp, softcover, $14.95

NEW! **DRUUNA: MORBUS GRAVIS I**
by Paolo Eleuteri Serpieri

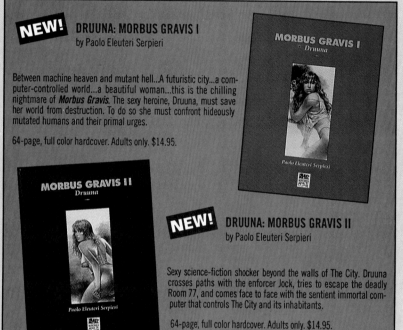

Between machine heaven and mutant hell...A futuristic city...a computer-controlled world...a beautiful woman...this is the chilling nightmare of *Morbus Gravis*. The sexy heroine, Druuna, must save her world from destruction. To do so she must confront hideously mutated humans and their primal urges.

64-page, full color hardcover. Adults only. $14.95.

NEW! **DRUUNA: MORBUS GRAVIS II**
by Paolo Eleuteri Serpieri

Sexy science-fiction shocker beyond the walls of The City. Druuna crosses paths with the enforcer Jock, tries to escape the deadly Room 77, and comes face to face with the sentient immortal computer that controls The City and its inhabitants.

64-page, full color hardcover. Adults only. $14.95.

CAPTAIN STERNN: Running Out of Time #1
by Bernie Wrightson

The long awaited return of Captain Sternn! Now you can get the first chapter of this five-part mini-series. See Captain Sternn, Beezer, Hanover Fiste, Filmore Coffers, beautiful women, the walking dead and great dinosaurs...as only Bernie Wrightson can do them.
48-page, full color comic, $4.95 per issue.

RUNNING OUT OF TIME

The Koalas of Australia

by Linda George

Content Consultant
Deborah Tabart, Executive Director
Australian Koala Foundation

Hilltop Books

An Imprint of Franklin Watts
A Division of Grolier Publishing
New Yo ; Sydney
Danbury, Connecticut

Hilltop Books
http://publishing.grolier.com
Copyright © 1998 by Capstone Press • All rights reserved
Published simultaneously in Canada • Printed in the United States of America

Library of Congress Cataloging-in-Publication Data
George, Linda.
   The koalas of Australia/by Linda George.
   p. cm.--(Animals of the world)
   Includes bibliographical references (p. 23) and index.
   Summary: Introduces the world of koalas, their physical characteristics,
   behavior, and interaction with humans.
   ISBN 1-56065-576-3
   1. Koala--Juvenile literature. [1. Koala.]
I. Title. II. Series.
QL737.M384G46   1998
599.2'5--dc21

                   97-11370
                    CIP
                    AC

Photo credits
Bob Bowdey, cover, 8
Michele Burgess, 20
FPG/Chris Michaels, 10; Travelpix, 12
Innerspace Visions/Doug Perrine, 16
Int'l Stock/Frank Grant, 4; Michele and Tom Grimm, 6
Lynn M. Stone, 14, 18

Table of Contents

About Koalas

Koalas are marsupials. A marsupial is a kind of animal. Female marsupials have pouches on their stomachs. Newborn marsupials live and grow in these pouches during their early lives.

Wild koalas live only in Australia. Australia is a continent in the South Pacific Ocean. A continent is one of the seven large land masses on earth.

Native Australians called Aborigines gave koalas their name. In the Aborigines' language, koala means does not drink. Koalas rarely drink water. They get the water they need from their food.

Male koalas weigh about 20 pounds (nine kilograms). Female koalas weigh about 14 pounds (six kilograms). Male koalas grow to be about three feet (90 centimeters) long. This measure is from the nose to the tail. Females are a little shorter.

Wild koalas live only in Australia.

What Koalas Look Like

Koalas have round faces with small, brown eyes. They have big, black noses and furry ears. Koalas also have small mouths with sharp teeth.

Koalas have the thickest fur of all marsupials. Most of their fur is brownish-gray. White fur grows on their stomachs and chins. Some white fur also grows on their ears.

Koalas have powerful front legs. They use them to climb trees. Koalas' back legs are the same length as their front legs.

Koalas have five toes on each foot. Each front foot has two toes that work like thumbs. Each back foot has one toe that works like a thumb. Koalas use these thumblike toes to grab food and hold onto tree branches.

Koalas have sharp claws on almost all their toes. The thumblike toes on their back feet do not have claws. Koalas use their claws to clean their fur. Sharp claws also help them climb trees.

Koalas use their front legs to climb trees.

Where Koalas Live

Wild koalas live in the eastern parts of Australia. The state of Queensland has the most koalas.

Koalas live in eucalyptus tree forests in Australia. Eucalyptus trees are gum trees that stay green all year. Gum is a sticky liquid inside the trees. Koalas eat the leaves and bark of eucalyptus trees.

There are more than 600 kinds of eucalyptus trees in Australia. Koalas eat from about 20 kinds of eucalyptus trees. The other trees are toxic to koalas. Toxic means harmful.

Each koala needs an area with 15 to 20 eucalyptus trees. The trees become toxic for a short time each year. But not all the trees become toxic at the same time. A koala moves to a different tree after one becomes toxic.

Koalas eat the leaves and bark of eucalyptus trees.

What Koalas Do

Koalas sleep or rest for about 18 hours each day. They sleep in the forks of eucalyptus trees. A fork is where two big branches come together. Koalas grip the trees tightly while they sleep. Sometimes koalas fall out of trees. But they are not usually hurt.

Koalas eat for about four hours every night. They sniff each leaf before they eat it. They can tell if leaves are toxic. If they are, koalas find other trees. Koalas also eat dirt to help them digest their food. Digest means to break down food so the body can use it.

Koalas spend nearly all their time in eucalyptus trees. They move very slowly in the trees. Koalas walk on the ground only to find new trees. Sometimes they jump from one tree to another.

Koalas sleep in the forks of eucalyptus trees.

Koala Enemies and Dangers

Koalas have only a few natural predators. A predator is an animal that hunts other animals for food. Wild dogs called dingoes sometimes attack koalas on the ground. Owls and lizards may attack young koalas. They attack when young koalas' mothers are away. Mother koalas try to protect their young.

Koalas' greatest enemies are people. Koalas are sometimes hit by cars. In Australia, road signs tell drivers to watch for koalas. But accidents still happen.

People also cut down eucalyptus trees to make room for houses and farms. Fewer eucalyptus trees means less food for koalas. Koalas in these areas may starve. Starve means to suffer or die from lack of food.

People sometimes start forest fires. Forest fires kill koalas. Fires kill eucalyptus trees, too.

Mother koalas try to protect their young.

Mating and Reproduction

Koalas mate between September and March. Mate means to join together to produce young. Female koalas are ready to mate when they are two years old. Male koalas are ready when they are three or four years old.

Male koalas mark trees during mating season. Mark means to leave a scent. A male koala rubs against a tree. Oil from its body comes off on the tree. This leaves the koala's scent on the tree. The scent tells other male koalas to stay away.

Male koalas also fight with other males during mating season. They fight for the attention of female koalas. Males call to females with low barking and grunting sounds. Females call to males with higher sounds.

Koalas mate in trees. Male koalas can mate with several females in a group. Female koalas give birth about 35 days after mating.

Male koalas mark trees during mating season.

Newborn and Young Koalas

A newborn koala weighs only one-thirtieth of an ounce (one gram). It is only three-fourths of an inch (about two centimeters) long. A newborn koala is pink and has no hair. It cannot see.

Somehow, the newborn koala finds its way to its mother's pouch. There it drinks its mother's milk. The young koala lives in the pouch for about six months.

The young koala then climbs out of its mother's pouch. It is about eight inches (20 centimeters) long at this time. The young koala holds onto the fur on its mother's chest. It stays out of the pouch for short periods of time. The mother feeds it partially digested leaves.

As it grows, the young koala begins to eat leaves on its own. It stays out of the pouch more. But it still stays close to its mother. After about one year, a young koala leaves its mother. It goes off to live on its own.

A young koala stays close to its mother.

Marsupials

Koalas belong to the marsupial family of animals. Many kinds of marsupials live in Australia. Among these are wallabies, wombats, and kangaroos. The opposums found in North America and South America are also marsupials.

The koala's closest relative is the wombat. Wombats look like koalas, but wombats are bigger. Wombats live in the mountain forests of Australia and Tasmania. Tasmania is an island near Australia in the Indian Ocean.

The kangaroo is another marsupial that lives in Australia. The kangaroo is much larger than the koala. It has long, powerful back legs. Kangaroo mothers carry young in their pouches for five to eight months.

The wombat is the koala's closest relative.

Koalas and People

Millions of koalas once lived in Australia. But people began hunting koalas for their fur in the early 1900s. Many koalas were killed during this time. People also cut down many eucalyptus trees. By 1927, only a few thousand koalas were left.

Some people feared there would be no more koalas. People passed laws to protect them. It is now against the law to kill koalas. But there are no laws protecting eucalyptus trees. Koalas need the trees to live.

Some koalas live in zoos. They can only live in zoos where eucalyptus trees can grow. Koalas born in zoos are sometimes returned to the wild. A few koalas live in zoos in the United States. Some koalas also live in zoos in Japan, Germany, and Portugal. People all over the world are working to help protect koalas.

Some koalas live in zoos.

Fast Facts

Common name: Koala

Scientific name: Phascolarctos cinereus

Life span: 13 to 18 years

Length: Adult male koalas are about three feet (90 centimeters) long from nose to tail. Females are shorter.

Weight: Newborn koalas weigh one-thirtieth of an ounce (one gram). Adult males weigh 20 pounds (nine kilograms). Adult females weigh 14 pounds (six kilograms).

Features: Koalas have thick, brownish-gray fur. They have strong front legs and sharp claws. Koalas use their toes like thumbs to grab food and climb trees.

Population: There are between 60,000 and 80,000 koalas in the wild.

Home: Koalas live in the eucalyptus tree forests of eastern Australia.

Habits: Koalas spend a lot of time in eucalyptus trees. They eat for about four hours each night. Adults live alone except when mating or caring for young.

Diet: Koalas eat eucalyptus leaves and bark.

Words to Know

Aborigines (ab-oh-RIH-jih-neez)—native people of Australia

Australia (aw-STRAYL-yuh)—a continent in the South Pacific Ocean

eucalyptus (yoo-kuh-LIP-tuhss)—a gum tree that stays green all year round

mammal (MAM-uhl)—a warm-blooded animal that has a backbone; baby mammals drink milk from their mothers' bodies

marsupial (mar-SOO-pee-uhl)—a kind of animal; female marsupials carry their young in a pouch on their stomach

predator (PRED-uh-tur)—an animal that hunts other animals for food

Read More

Arnold, Caroline. *Koala*. New York: Morrow, 1987.

Bright, Michael. *Koalas*. New York: Gloucester Press, 1990.

Hunt, Patricia. *Koalas*. New York: Dodd, Mead, 1980.

Useful Addresses

Lone Pine Koala Sanctuary
Jesmond Road
Fig Tree Pocket
Brisbane, Queensland 4069
Australia

Friends of the Koala
P.O. Box 5034
East Lismar, N.S.W. 2480
Australia

Internet Sites

Lone Pine Koala Sanctuary—Koala Information
http://www.koala.net/animals/koalas.htm

The Sydney Koala Park
http://www.anzac.com/aust/nsw/kp.htm

Index